Alfred Tennyson

Songs, etc. From the Published Writings of Alfred Tennyson

Alfred Tennyson

Songs, etc. From the Published Writings of Alfred Tennyson

ISBN/EAN: 9783337001780

Printed in Europe, USA, Canada, Australia, Japan

Cover: Foto ©Andreas Hilbeck / pixelio.de

More available books at **www.hansebooks.com**

SONGS

ETC.

From the Published Writings of

ALFRED TENNYSON, D.C.L.

POET-LAUREATE

Anchora Spei

STRAHAN & CO., PUBLISHERS

56 LUDGATE HILL, LONDON

1872

LONDON:
PRINTED BY VIRTUE AND CO.,
CITY ROAD.

CONTENTS.

FROM 'POEMS.'

FROM 'THE PRINCESS.'

CONTENTS. eXYZ

CONTENTS. vii

FROM 'IN MEMORIAM.'

FROM 'MAUD AND OTHER POEMS.'

FROM 'ENOCH ARDEN, ETC.'

FROM 'SELECTIONS.'

FROM 'IDYLLS OF THE KING.'

MARIANA.

WITH blackest moss the flower-plots
    Were thickly crusted, one and all :
    The rusted nails fell from the knots
That held the pear to the gable-wall.
The broken sheds look'd sad and strange :
    Unlifted was the clinking latch ;
    Weeded and worn the ancient thatch
Upon the lonely moated grange.

She only said, 'My life is dreary,
 He cometh not,' she said;
She said, 'I am aweary, aweary,
 I would that I were dead!'

Her tears fell with the dews at even;
 Her tears fell ere the dews were dried;
She could not look on the sweet heaven,
 Either at morn or eventide.
After the flitting of the bats,
 When thickest dark did trance the sky,
 She drew her casement-curtain by,
And glanced athwart the glooming flats.
 She only said, 'The night is dreary,
  He cometh not,' she said;

She said, ' I am aweary, aweary,
   I would that I were dead ! '

Upon the middle of the night,
   Waking she heard the night-fowl crow :
The cock sung out an hour ere light :
   From the dark fen the oxen's low
Came to her : without hope of change,
   In sleep she seem'd to walk forlorn,
   Till cold winds woke the gray-eyed morn
About the lonely moated grange.
     She only said, ' The day is dreary,
       He cometh not,' she said ;
     She said, ' I am aweary, aweary,
       I would that I were dead ! '

About a stone-cast from the wall
　A sluice with blacken'd waters slept,
And o'er it many, round and small,
　The cluster'd marish-mosses crept.
Hard by a poplar shook alway,
　All silver-green with gnarled bark:
For leagues no other tree did mark
The level waste, the rounding gray.
　　She only said, 'My life is dreary,
　　　He cometh not,' she said;
　　She said, 'I am aweary, aweary,
　　　I would that I were dead!'

And ever when the moon was low,
　And the shrill winds were up and away,

In the white curtain, to and fro,
 She saw the gusty shadow sway.
But when the moon was very low,
 And wild winds bound within their cell,
 The shadow of the poplar fell
Upon her bed, across her brow.
  She only said, 'The night is dreary,
   He cometh not,' she said;
  She said, 'I am aweary, aweary,
   I would that I were dead!'

All day within the dreamy house,
 The doors upon their hinges creak'd;
The blue fly sung in the pane; the mouse
 Behind the mouldering wainscot shriek'd,

Or from the crevice peer'd about.

    Old faces glimmer'd thro' the doors,

    Old footsteps trod the upper floors,

Old voices call'd her from without.

      She only said, ' My life is dreary,

        He cometh not,' she said ;

      She said, ' I am aweary, aweary,

        I would that I were dead !'

The sparrow's chirrup on the roof,

    The slow clock ticking, and the sound

Which to the wooing wind aloof

    The poplar made, did all confound

Her sense ; but most she loathed the hour

    When the thick-moted sunbeam lay

Athwart the chambers, and the day
Was sloping toward his western bower.
　　Then, said she, 'I am very dreary,
　　He will not come,' she said ;
　　She wept, 'I am aweary, aweary,
　　Oh God, that I were dead !'

THE SEA FAIRIES.

SLOW sail'd the weary mariners and
    saw,
  Betwixt the green brink and the
    running foam,
Sweet faces, rounded arms, and bosoms prest
To little harps of gold; and while they mused,
Whispering to each other half in fear,
Shrill music reach'd them on the middle sea.

Whither away, whither away, whither away ? fly
    no more.
Whither away from the high green field, and the
    happy blossoming shore ?
Day and night to the billow the fountain calls :
Down shower the gambolling waterfalls
From wandering over the lea :
Out of the live-green heart of the dells
They freshen the silvery-crimson shells,
And thick with white bells the clover-hill swells
High over the full-toned sea :
O hither, come hither and furl your sails,
Come hither to me and to me :
Hither, come hither and frolic and play ;
Here it is only the mew that wails ;
We will sing to you all the day :
Mariner, mariner, furl your sails,

For here are the blissful downs and dales,
And merrily merrily carol the gales,
And the spangle dances in bight and bay,
And the rainbow forms and flies on the land
Over the islands free ;
And the rainbow lives in the curve of the sand ;
Hither, come hither and see ;
And the rainbow hangs on the poising wave,
And sweet is the colour of cove and cave,
And sweet shall your welcome be :
O hither, come hither, and be our lords,
For merry brides are we :
We will kiss sweet kisses, and speak sweet
    words :
O listen, listen, your eyes shall glisten
With pleasure and love and jubilee :
O listen, listen, your eyes shall glisten

When the sharp clear twang of the golden chords
Runs up the ridged sea.
Who can light on as happy a shore
All the world o'er, all the world o'er?
Whither away? listen and stay: mariner, mariner,
    fly no more.

A DIRGE.

NOW is done thy long day's work;
    Fold thy palms across thy breast,
    Fold thine arms, turn to thy rest.
        Let them rave.
Shadows of the silver birk
Sweep the green that folds thy grave.
        Let them rave.

Thee nor carketh care nor slander;
Nothing but the small cold worm

Fretteth thine enshrouded form.

    Let them rave.

Light and shadow ever wander

O'er the green that folds thy grave.

    Let them rave.

Thou wilt not turn upon thy bed;

Chaunteth not the brooding bee

Sweeter tones than calumny?

    Let them rave.

Thou wilt never raise thine head

From the green that folds thy grave.

    Let them rave.

Crocodiles wept tears for thee;

The woodbine and eglatere

Drip sweeter dews than traitor's tear.
    Let them rave.
Rain makes music in the tree
O'er the green that folds thy grave.
    Let them rave.

Round thee blow, self-pleached deep,
Bramble roses, faint and pale,
And long purples of the dale.
    Let them rave.
These in every shower creep
Thro' the green that folds thy grave.
    Let them rave.

The gold-eyéd kingcups fine;
The frail bluebell peereth over

Rare broidry of the purple clover.

Let them rave.

Kings have no such couch as thine,

As the green that folds thy grave.

Let them rave.

Wild words wander here and there :

God's great gift of speech abused

Makes thy memory confused :

But let them rave.

The balm-cricket carols clear

In the green that folds thy grave.

Let them rave.

THE BALLAD OF ORIANA.

MY heart is wasted with my woe,
     Oriana.
There is no rest for me below,
     Oriana.
When the long dun wolds are ribb'd with snow,
And loud the Norland whirlwinds blow,
     Oriana,
Alone I wander to and fro,
     Oriana.

Ere the light on dark was growing,
     Oriana,
At midnight the cock was crowing,
     Oriana :
Winds were blowing, waters flowing,
We heard the steeds to battle going,
     Oriana ;
Aloud the hollow bugle blowing,
     Oriana.

In the yew-wood black as night,
     Oriana,
Ere I rode into the fight,
     Oriana,

C

While blissful tears blinded my sight
By star-shine and by moonlight,
      Oriana,
I to thee my troth did plight,
      Oriana.

She stood upon the castle wall,
      Oriana:
She watch'd my crest among them all,
      Oriana:
She saw me fight, she heard me call,
When forth there stept a foeman tall,
      Oriana,
Atween me and the castle wall,
      Oriana.

The bitter arrow went aside,
  Oriana :
The false, false arrow went aside,
  Oriana :
The damnéd arrow glanced aside,
And pierced thy heart, my love, my bride,
  Oriana !
Thy heart, my life, my love, my bride,
  Oriana !

Oh, narrow, narrow was the space,
  Oriana.
Loud, loud rung out the bugle's brays,
  Oriana.

Oh! deathful stabs were dealt apace,
The battle deepen'd in its place,
      Oriana;
But I was down upon my face,
      Oriana.

They should have stabb'd me where I lay,
      Oriana!
How could I rise and come away,
      Oriana?
How could I look upon the day?
They should have stabb'd me where I lay,
      Oriana—
They should have trod me into clay,
      Oriana.

O breaking heart that will not break,
> Oriana !
O pale, pale face so sweet and meek,
> Oriana !
Thou smilest, but thou dost not speak,
And then the tears run down my cheek,
> Oriana :
What wantest thou? whom dost thou seek,
> Oriana ?

I cry aloud: none hear my cries,
> Oriana.
Thou comest atween me and the skies,
> Oriana.

I feel the tears of blood arise
Up from my heart unto my eyes,
  Oriana.
Within thy heart my arrow lies,
  Oriana.

O cursed hand! O cursed blow!
  Oriana!
O happy thou that liest low,
  Oriana!
All night the silence seems to flow
Beside me in my utter woe,
  Oriana.
A weary, weary way I go,
  Oriana.

When Norland winds pipe down the sea,
>Oriana,
I walk, I dare not think of thee,
>Oriana.
Thou liest beneath the greenwood tree,
I dare not die and come to thee,
>Oriana.
I hear the roaring of the sea,
>Oriana.

THE MILLER'S DAUGHTER.

IT is the miller's daughter,
    And she is grown so dear, so dear,
That I would be the jewel
    That trembles at her ear:
For hid in ringlets day and night,
I'd touch her neck so warm and white.

And I would be the girdle
    About her dainty, dainty waist,

And her heart would beat against me,
   In sorrow and in rest :
And I should know if it beat right,
I'd clasp it round so close and tight.

And I would be the necklace,
   And all day long to fall and rise
Upon her balmy bosom,
   With her laughter or her sighs,
And I would lie so light, so light,
I scarce should be unclasp'd at night.

THE MILLER'S DAUGHTER.

LOVE that hath us in the net,
   Can he pass, and we forget?
   Many suns arise and set.
Many a chance the years beget.
Love the gift is Love the debt—
     Even so.

Love is hurt with jar and fret.
Love is made a vague regret.

Eyes with idle tears are wet.
Idle habit links us yet.
What is love? for we forget:
Ah, no! no!

THE SISTERS.

WE were two daughters of one race:
　　She was the fairest in the face:
　　　　The wind is blowing in turret and tree.
They were together, and she fell;
Therefore revenge became me well.
　　O the Earl was fair to see!

She died: she went to burning flame:
She mix'd her ancient blood with shame.

The wind is howling in turret and tree.
Whole weeks and months, and early and late,
To win his love I lay in wait:
   O the Earl was fair to see!

I made a feast; I bade him come;
I won his love, I brought him home.
   The wind is roaring in turret and tree.
And after supper, on a bed,
Upon my lap he laid his head:
   O the Earl was fair to see!

I kiss'd his eyelids into rest:
His ruddy cheek upon my breast.

The wind is raging in turret and tree.
I hated him with the hate of hell,
But I loved his beauty passing well.
　　O the Earl was fair to see!

I rose up in the silent night:
I made my dagger sharp and bright.
　　The wind is raving in turret and tree.
As half-asleep his breath he drew,
Three times I stabb'd him thro' and thro'.
　　O the Earl was fair to see!

I curl'd and comb'd his comely head,
He look'd so grand when he was dead.

The wind is blowing in turret and tree.
I wrapt his body in the sheet,
And laid him at his mother's feet.
    O the Earl was fair to see!

LADY CLARA VERE DE VERE.

LADY Clara Vere de Vere,
    Of me you shall not win renown :
    You thought to break a country heart
      For pastime, ere you went to town.
At me you smiled, but unbeguiled
    I saw the snare, and I retired :
The daughter of a hundred Earls,
    You are not one to be desired.

Lady Clara Vere de Vere,
  I know you proud to bear your name,
Your pride is yet no mate for mine,
  Too proud to care from whence I came.
Nor would I break for your sweet sake
  A heart that doats on truer charms.
A simple maiden in her flower
  Is worth a hundred coats-of-arms.

Lady Clara Vere de Vere,
  Some meeker pupil you must find,
For were you queen of all that is,
  I could not stoop to such a mind.
You sought to prove how I could love,
  And my disdain is my reply.

D

The lion on your old stone gates
 Is not more cold to you than I.

Lady Clara Vere de Vere,
 You put strange memories in my head.
Not thrice your branching limes have blown
 Since I beheld young Laurence dead.
Oh your sweet eyes, your low replies:
 A great enchantress you may be;
But there was that across his throat
 Which you had hardly cared to see.

Lady Clara Vere de Vere,
 When thus he met his mother's view,
She had the passions of her kind,
 She spake some certain truths of you.

Indeed I heard one bitter word
  That scarce is fit for you to hear ;
Her manners had not that repose
  Which stamps the caste of Vere de Vere.

Lady Clara Vere de Vere,
  There stands a spectre in your hall :
The guilt of blood is at your door :
  You changed a wholesome heart to gall.
You held your course without remorse,
  To make him trust his modest worth,
And, last, you fix'd a vacant stare,
  And slew him with your noble birth.

Trust me, Clara Vere de Vere,
  From yon blue heavens above us bent,

The grand old gardener and his wife
　Smile at the claims of long descent.
Howe'er it be, it seems to me,
　'Tis only noble to be good.
Kind hearts are more than coronets,
　And simple faith than Norman blood.

I know you, Clara Vere de Vere,
　You pine among your halls and towers :
The languid light of your proud eyes
　Is wearied of the rolling hours.
In glowing health, with boundless wealth,
　But sickening of a vague disease,
You know so ill to deal with time,
　You needs must play such pranks as these.

Clara, Clara Vere de Vere,
　　If Time be heavy on your hands,
Are there no beggars at your gate,
　　Nor any poor about your lands ?
Oh ! teach the orphan-boy to read,
　　Or teach the orphan-girl to sew,
Pray Heaven for a human heart,
　　And let the foolish yeoman go.

THE MAY QUEEN.

Y OU must wake and call me early, call me
early, mother dear;
To-morrow 'ill be the happiest time of all
the glad New-year;
Of all the glad New-year, mother, the maddest
merriest day;
For I'm to be Queen o' the May, mother, I'm to be
Queen o' the May.

There's many a black black eye, they say, but none
　　so bright as mine :

There's Margaret and Mary, there's Kate and
　　Caroline :

But none so fair as little Alice in all the land they
　　say,

So I'm to be Queen o' the May, mother, I'm to be
　　Queen o' the May.

I sleep so sound all night, mother, that I shall
　　never wake,

If you do not call me loud when the day begins to
　　break :

But I must gather knots of flowers, and buds and
　　garlands gay,

For I'm to be Queen o' the May, mother, I'm to be
Queen o' the May.

As I came up the valley whom think ye should I
see,
But Robin leaning on the bridge beneath the
hazel-tree ?
He thought of that sharp look, mother, I gave him
yesterday,—
But I'm to be Queen o' the May, mother, I'm to be
Queen o' the May.

He thought I was a ghost, mother, for I was all in
white,
And I ran by him without speaking, like a flash of
light.

They call me cruel-hearted, but I care not what
    they say,
For I'm to be Queen o' the May, mother, I'm to be
    Queen o' the May.

They say he's dying all for love, but that can never
    be :
They say his heart is breaking, mother—what is
    that to me ?
There's many a bolder lad 'ill woo me any summer
    day,
And I'm to be Queen o' the May, mother, I'm to be
    Queen o' the May.

Little Effie shall go with me to-morrow to the
    green,

And you'll be there, too, mother, to see me made
    the Queen ;
For the shepherd lads on every side 'ill come from
    far away,
And I'm to be Queen o' the May, mother, I'm to be
    Queen o' the May.

The honeysuckle round the porch has wov'n its
    wavy bowers,
And by the meadow-trenches blow the faint sweet
    cuckoo-flowers ;
And the wild marsh-marigold shines like fire in
    swamps and hollows gray,
And I'm to be Queen o' the May, mother, I'm to be
    Queen o' the May.

The night-winds come and go, mother, upon the
    meadow-grass,
And the happy stars above them seem to brighten
    as they pass;
There will not be a drop of rain the whole of the
    livelong day,
And I'm to be Queen o' the May, mother, I'm to be
    Queen o' the May.

All the valley, mother, 'ill be fresh and green and
    still,
And the cowslip and the crowfoot are over all the
    hill,
And the rivulet in the flowery dale 'ill merrily
    glance and play,

For I'm to be Queen o' the May, mother, I'm to be
Queen o' the May.

So you must wake and call me early, call me early,
mother dear,
To-morrow 'ill be the happiest time of all the glad
New-year :
To-morrow 'ill be of all the year the maddest
merriest day,
For I'm to be Queen o' the May, mother, I'm to be
Queen o' the May.

THE DEATH OF THE OLD YEAR.

FULL knee-deep lies the winter snow,
    And the winter winds are wearily
       sighing:
Toll ye the church-bell sad and slow,
And tread softly and speak low,
For the old year lies a-dying.
    Old year, you must not die:
    You came to us so readily,
    You lived with us so steadily,
    Old year, you shall not die.

He lieth still : he doth not move :
He will not see the dawn of day.
He hath no other life above.
He gave me a friend, and a true true-love,
And the New-year will take 'em away.
  Old year, you must not go ;
  So long as you have been with us,
  Such joy as you have seen with us,
  Old year, you shall not go.

He froth'd his bumpers to the brim ;
A jollier year we shall not see.
But tho' his eyes are waxing dim,
And tho' his foes speak ill of him,
He was a friend to me.

Old year, you shall not die;
We did so laugh and cry with you,
I've half a mind to die with you,
Old year, if you must die.

He was full of joke and jest,
But all his merry quips are o'er.
To see him die, across the waste
His son and heir doth ride post-haste,
But he'll be dead before.
　　Every one for his own.
　　The night is starry and cold, my friend,
　　And the New-year blithe and bold, my friend,
　　Comes up to take his own.

How hard he breathes! over the snow
I heard just now the crowing cock.

The shadows flicker to and fro :
The cricket chirps : the light burns low :
'Tis nearly twelve o'clock.
    Shake hands, before you die.
    Old year, we'll dearly rue for you :
    What is it we can do for you ?
    Speak out before you die.

His face is growing sharp and thin.
Alack ! our friend is gone.
Close up his eyes : tie up his chin :
Step from the corpse, and let him in
That standeth there alone,
    And waiteth at the door.
    There's a new foot on the floor, my friend,
    And a new face at the door, my friend,
    A new face at the door.

'OF OLD SAT FREEDOM ON THE HEIGHTS.'

OF old sat Freedom on the heights,
　　The thunders breaking at her feet:
　Above her shook the starry lights:
　　She heard the torrents meet.

There in her place she did rejoice,
　Self-gather'd in her prophet-mind,
But fragments of her mighty voice
　Came rolling on the wind.

E

Then stept she down thro' town and field
  To mingle with the human race,
And part by part to men reveal'd
  The fullness of her face—

Grave mother of majestic works,
  From her isle-altar gazing down,
Who, God-like, grasps the triple forks,
  And, King-like, wears the crown :

Her open eyes desire the truth.
  The wisdom of a thousand years
Is in them. May perpetual youth
  Keep dry their light from tears ;

That her fair form may stand and shine,
  Make bright our days and light our dreams,
Turning to scorn with lips divine
  The falsehood of extremes!

SONG FROM 'AUDLEY COURT.'

O H! who would fight and march and
countermarch,
    Be shot for sixpence in a battle-field,
And shovell'd up into some bloody trench
Where no one knows? but let me live my life.

Oh! who would cast and balance at a desk,
Perch'd like a crow upon a three-legg'd stool,
Till all his juice is dried, and all his joints
Are full of chalk? but let me live my life.

Who'd serve the state? for if I carved my name
Upon the cliffs that guard my native land,
I might as well have traced it in the sands;
The sea wastes all: but let me live my life.

Oh! who would love? I woo'd a woman once,
But she was sharper than an eastern wind,
And all my heart turn'd from her, as a thorn
Turns from the sea: but let me live my life.

'SLEEP, ELLEN AUBREY, SLEEP.'

SLEEP, Ellen Aubrey, sleep, and dream
of me :
Sleep, Ellen, folded in thy sister's arm,
And sleeping, haply dream her arm is mine.

Sleep, Ellen, folded in Emilia's arm ;
Emilia, fairer than all else but thou,
For thou art fairer than all else that is.

Sleep, breathing health and peace upon her breast :
Sleep, breathing love and trust against her lip :
I go to-night : I come to-morrow morn.

I go, but I return : I would I were
The pilot of the darkness and the dream.
Sleep, Ellen Aubrey, love, and dream of me.

THE GOLDEN YEAR.

WE sleep and wake and sleep, but all things
     move ;
     The Sun flies forward to his brother Sun ;
The dark Earth follows wheel'd in her ellipse ;
And human things returning on themselves   .
Move onward, leading up the golden year.

Ah, tho' the times, when some new thought can bud,
Are but as poets' seasons when they flower,

Yet seas, that daily gain upon the shore,
Have ebb and flow conditioning their march,
And slow and sure comes up the golden year.

When wealth no more shall rest in mounded heaps,
But smit with freër light shall slowly melt
In many streams to fatten lower lands,
And light shall spread, and man be liker man
Thro' all the season of the golden year.

Shall eagles not be eagles ? wrens be wrens ?
If all the world were falcons, what of that ?
The wonder of the eagle were the less,
But he not less the eagle. Happy days
Roll onward, leading up the golden year.

Fly, happy, happy sails, and bear the Press;
Fly happy with the mission of the Cross;
Knit land to land, and blowing havenward
With silks, and fruits, and spices, clear of toll,
Enrich the markets of the golden year.

But we grow old. Ah! when shall all men's good
Be each man's rule, and universal Peace
Lie like a shaft of light across the land,
And like a lane of beams athwart the sea
Thro' all the circle of the golden year.

THE DAY DREAM: THE DEPARTURE.

AND on her lover's arm she leant,
    And round her waist she felt it fold,
    And far across the hills they went
      In that new world which is the old :
Across the hills, and far away
    Beyond their utmost purple rim,
And deep into the dying day
    The happy princess follow'd him.

' I'd sleep another hundred years,
   O love, for such another kiss ; '
' O wake for ever, love,' she hears,
   ' O love, 'twas such as this and this.'
And o'er them many a sliding star,
   And many a merry wind was borne,
And, stream'd thro' many a golden bar,
   The twilight melted into morn.

' O eyes long laid in happy sleep ! '
   ' O happy sleep, that lightly fled ! '
' O happy kiss, that woke thy sleep ! '
   ' O love, thy kiss would wake the dead ! '
And o'er them many a flowing range
   Of vapour buoy'd the crescent-bark,

And, rapt thro' many a rosy change,
　　The twilight died into the dark.

'A hundred summers ! can it be ?
　　And whither goest thou, tell me where ?'
'O seek my father's court with me,
　　For there are greater wonders there.'
And o'er the hills, and far away
　　Beyond their utmost purple rim,
Beyond the night, across the day,
　　Thro' all the world she follow'd him.

ST. AGNES EVE.

DEEP on the convent-roof the snows
    Are sparkling to the moon :
My breath to heaven like vapour goes :
    May my soul follow soon !
The shadows of the convent-towers
    Slant down the snowy sward,
Still creeping with the creeping hours
    That lead me to my Lord :
Make Thou my spirit pure and clear
    As are the frosty skies,

Or this first snowdrop of the year
  That in my bosom lies.

As these white robes are soil'd and dark,
  To yonder shining ground;
As this pale taper's earthly spark,
  To yonder argent round;
So shows my soul before the Lamb,
  My spirit before Thee;
So in mine earthly house I am,
  To that I hope to be.
Break up the heavens, O Lord! and far,
  Thro' all yon starlight keen,
Draw me, thy bride, a glittering star
  In raiment white and clean.

He lifts me to the golden doors;
   The flashes come and go;
All heaven bursts her starry floors,
   And strows her lights below,
And deepens on and up! the gates
   Roll back, and far within
For me the Heavenly Bridegroom waits,
   To make me pure of sin.
The sabbaths of Eternity,
   One sabbath deep and wide—
A light upon the shining sea—
   The Bridegroom with his bride!

EDWARD GRAY.

SWEET Emma Moreland of yonder town
    Met me walking on yonder way,
'And have you lost your heart?' she
    said :
'And are you married yet, Edward Gray?'

Sweet Emma Moreland spoke to me :
    Bitterly weeping I turn'd away :
'Sweet Emma Moreland, love no more
    Can touch the heart of Edward Gray.

F

' Ellen Adair she loved me well,
    Against her father's and mother's will :
To-day I sat for an hour and wept,
    By Ellen's grave, on the windy hill.

' Shy she was, and I thought her cold ;
    Thought her proud, and fled over the sea ;
Fill'd I was with folly and spite,
    When Ellen Adair was dying for me.

' Cruel, cruel the words I said !
    Cruelly came they back to-day :
" You're too slight and fickle," I said,
    " To trouble the heart of Edward Gray."

'There I put my face in the grass—
   Whisper'd " Listen to my despair :
I repent me of all I did.
   Speak a little, Ellen Adair!"

'Then I took a pencil, and wrote
   On the mossy stone, as I lay,
" Here lies the body of Ellen Adair ;
   And here the heart of Edward Gray !"

'Love may come, and love may go,
   And fly, like a bird, from tree to tree :
But I will love no more, no more,
   Till Ellen Adair come back to me.

'Bitterly wept I over the stone :
   Bitterly weeping I turn'd away :
There lies the body of Ellen Adair !
   And there the heart of Edward Gray !'

A FAREWELL.

FLOW down, cold rivulet, to the sea,
   Thy tribute wave deliver :
No more by thee my steps shall be,
   For ever and for ever.

Flow, softly flow, by lawn and lea,
   A rivulet then a river :
Nowhere by thee my steps shall be,
   For ever and for ever.

But here will sigh thine alder tree,
　　And here thine aspen shiver;
And here by thee will hum the bee,
　　For ever and for ever.

A thousand suns will stream on thee,
　　A thousand moons will quiver;
But not by thee my steps shall be,
　　For ever and for ever.

THE BEGGAR MAID.

HER arms across her breast she laid;
　　She was more fair than words can say:
　Barefooted came the beggar maid
　　Before the king Cophetua.
In robe and crown the king stept down,
　To meet and greet her on her way;
'It is no wonder,' said the lords,
　'She is more beautiful than day.'

As shines the moon in clouded skies,
　She in her poor attire was seen :
One praised her ankles, one her eyes,
　One her dark hair and lovesome mien.
So sweet a face, such angel grace,
　In all that land had never been :
Cophetua sware a royal oath :
　' This beggar maid shall be my queen ! '

'COME NOT WHEN I AM DEAD.'

COME not, when I am dead,
    To drop thy foolish tears upon my
        grave,
To trample round my fallen head,
  And vex the unhappy dust thou wouldst not save.
There let the wind sweep and the plover cry;
    But thou, go by.

Child, if it were thine error or thy crime
  I care no longer, being all unblest :

Wed whom thou wilt, but I am sick of Time,
  And I desire to rest.
Pass on, weak heart, and leave me where I lie:
  Go by, go by.

'MOVE EASTWARD, HAPPY EARTH.'

MOVE eastward, happy earth, and leave
    Yon orange sunset waning slow;
    From fringes of the faded eve,
      O, happy planet, eastward go :
Till over thy dark shoulder glow
    Thy silver sister-world, and rise
    To glass herself in dewy eyes
That watch me from the glen below.

Ah, bear me with thee, smoothly borne,
Dip forward under starry light,
And move me to my marriage-morn,
And round again to happy night.

'BREAK, BREAK, BREAK.'

BREAK, break, break,
   On thy cold gray stones, O Sea!
And I would that my tongue could utter
   The thoughts that arise in me.

O well for the fisherman's boy,
   That he shouts with his sister at play!
O well for the sailor lad,
   That he sings in his boat on the bay!

And the stately ships go on
 To their haven under the hill;
But O for the touch of a vanish'd hand,
 And the sound of a voice that is still!

Break, break, break,
 At the foot of thy crags, O Sea!
But the tender grace of a day that is dead
 Will never come back to me.

THE POET'S SONG.

THE rain had fallen, the Poet arose,
    He pass'd by the town and out of the
       street,
A light wind blew from the gates of the sun,
  And waves of shadow went over the wheat,
And he sat him down in a lonely place,
  And chanted a melody loud and sweet,
That made the wild-swan pause in her cloud,
  And the lark drop down at his feet.

The swallow stopt as he hunted the bee,
   The snake slipt under a spray,
The wild hawk stood with the down on his beak,
   And stared, with his foot on the prey,
And the nightingale thought, 'I have sung many
      songs,
   But never a one so gay,
For he sings of what the world will be
   When the years have died away.'

'AS THROUGH THE LAND AT EVE WE WENT.'

AS thro' the land at eve we went,
    And pluck'd the ripen'd ears,
    We fell out, my wife and I,
O we fell out I know not why,
  And kiss'd again with tears.

And blessings on the falling out
  That all the more endears,

When we fall out with those we love,
   And kiss again with tears!

For when we came where lies the child
   We lost in other years,
There above the little grave,
O there above the little grave,
   We kiss'd again with tears.

'SWEET AND LOW, SWEET AND LOW.'

SWEET and low, sweet and low,
　　Wind of the western sea,
　　Low, low, breathe and blow,
　　Wind of the western sea!
　Over the rolling waters go,
　Come from the dying moon, and blow,
　　Blow him again to me;
While my little one, while my pretty one, sleeps.

Sleep and rest, sleep and rest,
    Father will come to thee soon ;
Rest, rest, on mother's breast,
    Father will come to thee soon ;
Father will come to his babe in the nest,
Silver sails all out of the west
    Under the silver moon :
Sleep, my little one, sleep, my pretty one, sleep.

'THE SPLENDOUR FALLS ON CASTLE WALLS.'

THE splendour falls on castle walls
  And snowy summits old in story:
  The long light shakes across the lakes
  And the wild cataract leaps in glory.
Blow, bugle, blow, set the wild echoes flying,
Blow, bugle; answer, echoes, dying, dying, dying.

 O hark, O hear! how thin and clear,
  And thinner, clearer, farther going!

O sweet and far from cliff and scar
   The horns of Elfland faintly blowing!
Blow, let us hear the purple glens replying:
Blow, bugle; answer, echoes, dying, dying, dying.

O love, they die in yon rich sky,
   They faint on hill or field or river:
Our echoes roll from soul to soul,
   And grow for ever and for ever.
Blow, bugle, blow, set the wild echoes flying,
And answer, echoes, answer, dying, dying, dying.

'TEARS, IDLE TEARS, I KNOW NOT WHAT THEY MEAN.'

TEARS, idle tears, I know not what they
    mean,
    Tears from the depth of some divine
    despair
Rise in the heart, and gather to the eyes,
In looking on the happy Autumn-fields,
And thinking of the days that are no more.

Fresh as the first beam glittering on a sail,
That brings our friends up from the underworld,

Sad as the last which reddens over one
That sinks with all we love below the verge;
So sad, so fresh, the days that are no more.

Ah, sad and strange as in dark summer dawns
The earliest pipe of half-awaken'd birds
To dying ears, when unto dying eyes
The casement slowly grows a glimmering square;
So sad, so strange, the days that are no more.

Dear as remember'd kisses after death,
And sweet as those by hopeless fancy feign'd
On lips that are for others; deep as love,
Deep as first love, and wild with all regret;
O Death in Life, the days that are no more.

'O SWALLOW, SWALLOW, FLYING, FLYING SOUTH.'

 SWALLOW, Swallow, flying, flying
South,
Fly to her, and fall upon her gilded
eaves,
And tell her, tell her, what I tell to thee.

O tell her Swallow, thou that knowest each,
That bright and fierce and fickle is the South,
And dark and true and tender is the North.

O Swallow, Swallow, if I could follow, and light
Upon her lattice, I would pipe and trill,
And cheep and twitter twenty million loves.

O were I thou that she might take me in,
And lay me on her bosom, and her heart
Would rock the snowy cradle till I died.

Why lingereth she to clothe her heart with love,
Delaying as the tender ash delays
To clothe herself, when all the woods are green ?

O tell her, Swallow, that thy brood is flown :
Say to her, I do but wanton in the South,
But in the North long since my nest is made.

O tell her, brief is life, but love is long,

And brief the sun of summer in the North,

And brief the moon of beauty in the South.

O Swallow, flying from the golden woods,

Fly to her, and pipe and woo her, and make her
    mine,

And tell her, tell her, that I follow thee.

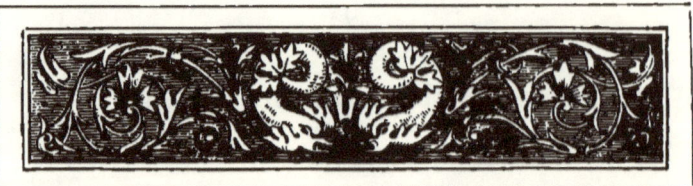

'THY VOICE IS HEARD THROUGH ROLLING DRUMS.'

THY voice is heard thro' rolling drums,
  That beat to battle where he stands;
Thy face across his fancy comes,
  And gives the battle to his hands:
A moment, while the trumpets blow,
  He sees his brood about thy knee;
The next like fire he meets the foe,
  And strikes him dead for thine and thee.

'HOME THEY BROUGHT HER WARRIOR DEAD.'

HOME they brought her warrior dead :
    She nor swoon'd, nor utter'd cry :
    All her maidens, watching, said,
 'She must weep or she will die.'

    Then they praised him, soft and low,
      Call'd him worthy to be loved,
    Truest friend and noblest foe ;
      Yet she neither spoke nor moved.

Stole a maiden from her place,
 Lightly to the warrior stept,
Took the face-cloth from the face;
 Yet she neither moved nor wept.

Rose a nurse of ninety years—
 Set his child upon her knee—
Like summer tempest came her tears—
 'Sweet my child, I live for thee.'

'OUR ENEMIES HAVE FALL'N, HAVE FALL'N.'

OUR enemies have fall'n, have fall'n; the
  seed,
 The little seed they laugh'd at in the
  dark,
Has risen and cleft the soil, and grown a bulk
Of spanless girth, that lays on every side
A thousand arms and rushes to the Sun.

Our enemies have fall'n, have fall'n : they came;
The leaves were wet with women's tears: they
  heard

A noise of songs they would not understand :
They mark'd it with the red cross to the fall,
And would have strown it, and are fall'n themselves.

Our enemies have fall'n, have fall'n : they came,
The woodmen with their axes : lo the tree !
But we will make it faggots for the hearth,
And shape it plank and beam for roof and floor,
And boats and bridges for the use of men.

Our enemies have fall'n, have fall'n : they struck ;
With their own blows they hurt themselves, nor
        knew
There dwelt an iron nature in the grain :

The glittering axe was broken in their arms,
Their arms were shatter'd to the shoulder blade.

Our enemies have fall'n, but this shall grow
A night of Summer from the heat, a breadth
Of Autumn, dropping fruits of power ; and roll'd
With music in the growing breeze of Time,
The tops shall strike from star to star, the fangs
Shall move the stony bases of the world.

H

'ASK ME NO MORE.'

ASK me no more : the moon may draw the
 sea ;
The cloud may stoop from heaven and
 take the shape,
With fold to fold, of mountain or of cape ;
But O too fond, when have I answer'd thee ?
 Ask me no more.

Ask me no more : what answer should I give ?
I love not hollow cheek or faded eye :

Yet, O my friend, I will not have thee die !
Ask me no more, lest I should bid thee live ;
      Ask me no more.

Ask me no more : thy fate and mine are seal'd :
  I strove against the stream and all in vain :
  Let the great river take me to the main :
No more, dear love, for at a touch I yield ;
      Ask me no more.

'NOW SLEEPS THE CRIMSON PETAL, NOW THE WHITE.'

NOW sleeps the crimson petal, now the
    white ;
Nor waves the cypress in the palace
    walk ;
Nor winks the gold fin in the porphyry font :
The firefly wakens : waken thou with me.

Now droops the milkwhite peacock like a ghost,
And like a ghost she glimmers on to me.

Now lies the Earth all Danaë to the stars,
And all thy heart lies open unto me.

Now slides the silent meteor on, and leaves
A shining furrow, as thy thoughts in me.

Now folds the lily all her sweetness up,
And slips into the bosom of the lake :
So fold thyself, my dearest, thou, and slip
Into my bosom and be lost in me.

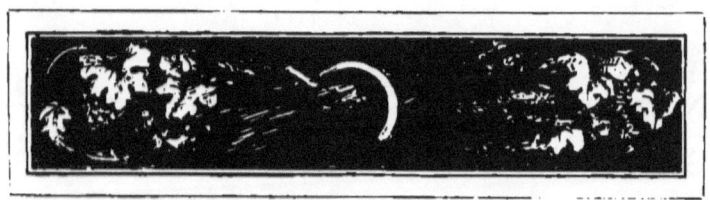

'COME DOWN, O MAID, FROM YONDER MOUNTAIN HEIGHT.'

OME down, O maid, from yonder moun-
tain height:
What pleasure lives in height (the shep-
herd sang),
In height and cold, the splendour of the hills ?
But cease to move so near the Heavens, and cease
To glide a sunbeam by the blasted Pine,
To sit a star upon the sparkling spire ;
And come, for Love is of the valley, come,
For Love is of the valley, come thou down

And find him; by the happy threshold, he,
Or hand in hand with Plenty in the maize,
Or red with spirted purple of the vats,
Or foxlike in the vine; nor cares to walk
With Death and Morning on the silver horns,
Nor wilt thou snare him in the white ravine,
Nor find him dropt upon the firths of ice,
That huddling slant in furrow-cloven falls
To roll the torrent out of dusky doors :
But follow; let the torrent dance thee down
To find him in the valley; let the wild
Lean-headed Eagles yelp alone, and leave
The monstrous ledges there to slope, and spill
Their thousand wreaths of dangling water-smoke,
That like a broken purpose waste in air :
So waste not thou; but come; for all the vales
Await thee; azure pillars of the hearth

Arise to thee; the children call, and I
Thy shepherd pipe, and sweet is every sound,
Sweeter thy voice, but every sound is sweet;
Myriads of rivulets hurrying thro' the lawn,
The moan of doves in immemorial elms,
And murmuring of innumerable bees.

'RING OUT, WILD BELLS.'

RING out, wild bells, to the wild sky,
 The flying cloud, the frosty light :
 The year is dying in the night ;
Ring out, wild bells, and let him die.

Ring out the old, ring in the new,
 Ring, happy bells, across the snow :
 The year is going, let him go ;
Ring out the false, ring in the true.

Ring out the grief that saps the mind,
    For those that here, we see no more;
    Ring out the feud of rich and poor,
Ring in redress to all mankind.

Ring out a slowly dying cause,
    And ancient forms of party strife;
    Ring in the nobler modes of life,
With sweeter manners, purer laws.

Ring out the want, the care, the sin,
    The faithless coldness of the times;
    Ring out, ring out my mournful rhymes,
But ring the fuller minstrel in.

Ring out false pride in place and blood,
    The civic slander and the spite ;
    Ring in the love of truth and right,
Ring in the common love of good.

Ring out old shapes of foul disease ;
    Ring out the narrowing lust of gold ;
    Ring out the thousand wars of old,
Ring in the thousand years·of peace.

Ring in the valiant man and free,
    The larger heart, the kindlier hand ;
    Ring out the darkness of the land,
Ring in the Christ that is to be.

'A VOICE BY THE CEDAR TREE.'

 VOICE by the cedar tree,
In the meadow under the Hall!
She is singing an air that is known
to me,
A passionate ballad gallant and gay,
A martial song like a trumpet's call!
Singing alone in the morning of life,
In the happy morning of life and of May,
Singing of men that in battle array,
Ready in heart and ready in hand,

March with banner and bugle and fife
To the death, for their native land.

Maud with her exquisite face,
And wild voice pealing up to the sunny sky,
And feet like sunny gems on an English green,
Maud in the light of her youth and her grace,
Singing of Death, and of Honour that cannot die,
Till I well could weep for a time so sordid and
mean,
And myself so languid and base.

Silence, beautiful voice!
Be still, for you only trouble the mind
With a joy in which I cannot rejoice,
A glory I shall not find.

Still! I will hear you no more,
For your sweetness hardly leaves me a choice
But to move to the meadow and fall before
Her feet on the meadow grass, and adore,
Not her, who is neither courtly nor kind,
Not her, not her, but a voice.

'O LET THE SOLID GROUND.'

O LET the solid ground
　　Not fail beneath my feet
Before my life has found
　　What some have found so sweet;
Then let come what come may,
What matter if I go mad,
I shall have had my day.

Let the sweet heavens endure,
　　Not close and darken above me

Before I am quite quite sure
　　That there is one to love me ;
Then let come what come may
To a life that has been so sad,
I shall have had my day.

'BIRDS IN THE HIGH HALL-GARDEN.'

BIRDS in the high Hall-garden
    When twilight was falling,
Maud, Maud, Maud, Maud,
    They were crying and calling.

Where was Maud ? in our wood ;
    And I, who else, was with her,
Gathering woodland lilies,
    Myriads blow together.

I

Birds in our wood sang
   Ringing thro' the valleys,
Maud is here, here, here
   In among the lilies.

I kiss'd her slender hand,
   She took the kiss sedately ;
Maud is not seventeen,
   But she is tall and stately.

I to cry out on pride
   Who have won her favour !
O Maud were sure of Heaven
   If lowliness could save her.

I know the way she went
   Home with her maiden posy,
For her feet have touch'd the meadows
   And left the daisies rosy.

Birds in the high Hall-garden
   Were crying and calling to her,
Where is Maud, Maud, Maud?
   One is come to woo her.

Look, a horse at the door,
   And little King Charlie snarling,
Go back, my lord, across the moor,
   You are not her darling.

'GO NOT, HAPPY DAY.'

GO not, happy day,
    From the shining fields,
Go not, happy day,
    Till the maiden yields.
Rosy is the West,
    Rosy is the South,
Roses are her cheeks,
    And a rose her mouth.
When the happy Yes
    Falters from her lips,
Pass and blush the news
    Over glowing ships;

Over blowing seas,
　Over seas at rest,
Pass the happy news,
　Blush it thro' the West;
Till the red man dance
　By his red cedar-tree,
And the red man's babe
　Leap, beyond the sea.
Blush from West to East,
　Blush from East to West;
Till the West is East,
　Blush it thro' the West.
Rosy is the West,
　Rosy is the South,
Roses are her cheeks,
　And a rose her mouth.

'COME INTO THE GARDEN, MAUD.'

COME into the garden, Maud,
    For the black bat, night, has flown,
    Come into the garden, Maud,
      I am here at the gate alone;
And the woodbine spices are wafted abroad,
    And the musk of the roses blown.

For a breeze of morning moves,
    And the planet of Love is on high,

Beginning to faint in the light that she loves,
  On a bed of daffodil sky,
To faint in the light of the sun she loves,
  To faint in his light, and to die.

All night have the roses heard
  The flute, violin, bassoon ;
All night has the casement jessamine stirr'd
  To the dancers dancing in tune ;
Till a silence fell with the waking bird,
  And a hush with the setting moon.

I said to the lily, ' There is but one
  With whom she has heart to be gay.
When will the dancers leave her alone ?
  She is weary of dance and play.'

Now half to the setting moon are gone,
   And half to the rising day;
Low on the sand and loud on the stone
   The last wheel echoes away.

I said to the rose, 'The brief night goes
   In babble and revel and wine.
O young lord-lover, what sighs are those,
   For one that will never be thine?
But mine, but mine,' so I sware to the rose,
   'For ever and ever, mine.'

And the soul of the rose went into my blood,
   As the music clash'd in the hall;
And long by the garden lake I stood,
   For I heard your rivulet fall

From the lake to the meadow and on to the wood,
   Our wood, that is dearer than all.

From the meadow your walks have left so sweet
   That whenever a March-wind sighs
He sets the jewel-print of your feet
   In violets blue as your eyes,
To the woody hollows in which we meet
   And the valleys of Paradise.

The slender acacia would not shake
   One long milk-bloom on the tree ;
The white lake-blossom fell into the lake,
   As the pimpernel dozed on the lea ;
But the rose was awake all night for your sake,
   Knowing your promise to me ;

The lilies and roses were all awake,
　　They sigh'd for the dawn and thee.

Queen rose of the rosebud garden of girls,
　　Come hither, the dances are done,
In gloss of satin and glimmer of pearls,
　　Queen lily and rose in one ;
Shine out, little head, sunning over with curls,
　　To the flowers, and be their sun.

There has fallen a splendid tear
　　From the passion-flower at the gate.
She is coming, my dove, my dear ;
　　She is coming, my life, my fate ;
The red rose cries, ‘ She is near, she is near ;’
　　And the white rose weeps, ‘ She is late ; ’

The larkspur listens, 'I hear, I hear;'
And the lily whispers, 'I wait.'

She is coming, my own, my sweet;
　Were it ever so airy a tread,
My heart would hear her and beat,
　Were it earth in an earthy bed;
My dust would hear her and beat,
　Had I lain for a century dead;
Would start and tremble under her feet,
　And blossom in purple and red.

THE BROOK.

COME from haunts of coot and hern,
   I make a sudden sally
And sparkle out among the fern,
   To bicker down a valley.

By thirty hills I hurry down,
   Or slip between the ridges,
By twenty thorps, a little town,
   And half a hundred bridges.

Till last by Philip's farm I flow
   To join the brimming river,
For men may come and men may go,
   But I go on for ever.

II.

I chatter over stony ways,
   In little sharps and trebles,
I bubble into eddying bays,
   I babble on the pebbles.

With many a curve my banks I fret
   By many a field and fallow,
And many a fairy foreland set
   With willow-weed and mallow.

I chatter, chatter, as I flow
   To join the brimming river,
For men may come and men may go,
   But I go on for ever.

III.

I wind about, and in and out,
   With here a blossom sailing,
And here and there a lusty trout,
   And here and there a grayling,

And here and there a foamy flake
   Upon me, as I travel
With many a silvery waterbreak
   Above the golden gravel,

And draw them all along, and flow
  To join the brimming river,
For men may come and men may go,
  But I go on for ever.

IV.

I steal by lawns and grassy plots,
  I slide by hazel covers;
I move the sweet forget-me-nots
  That grow for happy lovers.

I slip, I slide, I gloom, I glance,
  Among my skimming swallows;
I make the netted sunbeam dance
  Against my sandy shallows.

I murmur under moon and stars
  In brambly wildernesses ;
I linger by my shingly bars ;
  I loiter round my cresses ;

And out again I curve and flow
  To join the brimming river,
For men may come and men may go,
  But I go on for ever.

THE CHARGE OF THE LIGHT BRIGADE.

HALF a league, half a league,
  Half a league onward,
All in the valley of Death
  Rode the six hundred.
"Forward, the Light Brigade!
Charge for the guns!" he said:
Into the valley of Death
  Rode the six hundred.

K

" Forward, the Light Brigade ! "
Was there a man dismay'd ?
Not tho' the soldier knew
   Some one had blunder'd :
Theirs not to make reply,
Theirs not to reason why,
Theirs but to do and die :
· Into the valley of Death
   Rode the six hundred.

Cannon to right of them,
Cannon to left of them,
Cannon in front of them
   Volley'd and thunder'd ;
Storm'd at with shot and shell,

Boldly they rode and well,
Into the jaws of Death,
Into the mouth of Hell
  Rode the six hundred.

Flash'd all their sabres bare,
Flash'd as they turn'd in air,
Sabring the gunners there,
Charging an army, while
  All the world wonder'd :
Plunged in the battery-smoke
Right thro' the line they broke ;
Cossack and Russian
Reel'd from the sabre-stroke
  Shatter'd and sunder'd.

Then they rode back, but not
    Not the six hundred.

Cannon to right of them,
Cannon to left of them,
Cannon behind them
    Volley'd and thunder'd ;
Storm'd at with shot and shell,
While horse and hero fell,
They that had fought so well
Came thro' the jaws of Death
Back from the mouth of Hell,
All that was left of them,
    Left of six hundred.

When can their glory fade?
O the wild charge they made!
　All the world wonder'd.
Honour the charge they made!
Honour the Light Brigade,
　Noble six hundred!

CRADLE-SONG.

WHAT does little birdie say
In her nest at peep of day?
Let me fly, says little birdie,
Mother, let me fly away.
Birdie, rest a little longer,
Till the little wings are stronger.
So she rests a little longer,
Then she flies away.

What does little baby say,
In her bed at peep of day?
Baby says, like little birdie,
Let me rise and fly away.
Baby, sleep a little longer,
Till the little limbs are stronger.
If she sleeps a little longer,
Baby too shall fly away.

IN THE VALLEY OF CAUTERETZ.

ALL along the valley, stream that flashest
    white,
  Deepening thy voice with the deepening
    of the night,
All along the valley, where thy waters flow,
I walk'd with one I loved two and thirty years ago.
All along the valley, while I walk'd to-day,
The two and thirty years were a mist that rolls
    away;

For all along the valley, down thy rocky bed
Thy living voice to me was as the voice of the dead,
And all along the valley, by rock and cave and tree,
The voice of the dead was a living voice to me.

THE SAILOR BOY.

HE rose at dawn and, fired with hope,
  Shot o'er the seething harbour-bar,
And reach'd the ship and caught the
    rope,
And whistled to the morning star.

And while he whistled long and loud
He heard a fierce mermaiden cry,

'O boy, tho' thou art young and proud,
   I see the place where thou wilt lie.

'The sands and yeasty surges mix
   In caves about the dreary bay,
And on thy ribs the limpet sticks,
   And in thy heart the scrawl shall play.'

'Fool,' he answer'd, 'death is sure
   To those that stay and those that roam,
But I will nevermore endure
   To sit with empty hands at home.

'My mother clings about my neck,
   My sisters crying, "Stay for shame;"

My father raves of death and wreck,
   They are all to blame, they are all to blame.

'God help me! save I take my part
   Of danger on the roaring sea,
A devil rises in my heart,
   Far worse than any death to me.'

THE ISLET.

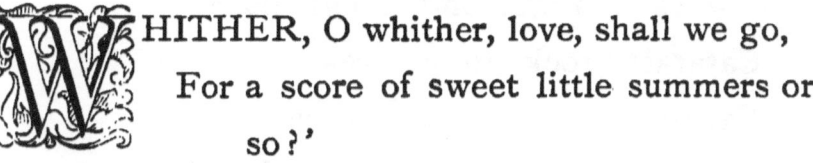HITHER, O whither, love, shall we go,
  For a score of sweet little summers or
    so?'
The sweet little wife of the singer said,
On the day that follow'd the day she was wed,
'Whither, O whither, love, shall we go?'
And the singer shaking his curly head
Turn'd as he sat, and struck the keys
There at his right with a sudden crash,
Singing, 'And shall it be over the seas
With a crew that is neither rude nor rash,

But a bevy of Eroses apple-cheek'd,
In a shallop of crystal ivory-beak'd,
With a satin sail of a ruby glow,
To a sweet little Eden on earth that I know,
A mountain islet pointed and peak'd;
Waves on a diamond shingle dash,
Cataract brooks to the ocean run,
Fairily-delicate palaces shine
Mixt with myrtle and clad with vine,
And overstream'd and silvery-streak'd
With many a rivulet high against the Sun
The facets of the glorious mountain flash
Above the valleys of palm and pine.'

'Thither, O thither, love, let us go.'

'No, no, no!

For in all that exquisite isle, my dear,
There is but one bird with a musical throat,
And his compass is but of a single note,
That it makes one weary to hear.'

'Mock me not! mock me not! love, let us go.'

"No, love, no.
For the bud ever breaks into bloom on the tree,
And a storm never wakes on the lonely sea,
And a worm is there in the lonely wood,
That pierces the liver and blackens the blood;
And makes it a sorrow to be."

A WELCOME TO ALEXANDRA.

SEA-KINGS' daughter from over the sea,
    Alexandra!
Saxon and Norman and Dane are we,
But all of us Danes in our welcome of thee,
    Alexandra!
Welcome her, thunders of fort and of fleet!
Welcome her, thundering cheer of the street!
Welcome her, all things youthful and sweet,
Scatter the blossom under her feet!

Break, happy land, into earlier flowers!

Make music, O bird, in the new-budded bowers!

Blazon your mottos of blessing and prayer!

Welcome her, welcome her, all that is ours!

Warble, O bugle, and trumpet, blare!

Flags, flutter out upon turrets and towers!

Flames, on the windy headland flare!

Utter your jubilee, steeple and spire!

Clash, ye bells, in the merry March air!

Flash, ye cities, in rivers of fire!

Rush to the roof, sudden rocket, and higher

Melt into stars for the land's desire!

Roll and rejoice, jubilant voice,

Roll as a ground-swell dash'd on the strand,

Roar as the sea when he welcomes the land,

And welcome her, welcome the land's desire,

The sea-kings' daughter as happy as fair,

L

Blissful bride of a blissful heir,

Bride of the heir of the kings of the sea—

O joy to the people and joy to the throne,

Come to us, love us and make us your own :

For Saxon or Dane or Norman we,

Teuton or Celt, or whatever we be,

We are each all Dane in our welcome of thee,

Alexandra !

'HOME THEY BROUGHT HIM, SLAIN WITH SPEARS.'

HOME they brought him slain with spears.
    They brought him home at even-fall :
All alone she sits and hears
    Echoes in his empty hall,
      Sounding on the morrow.

The Sun peep'd in from open field,
    The boy began to leap and prance,
    Rode upon his father's lance,
Beat upon his father's shield—
      'O hush, my joy, my sorrow.'

MERLIN'S SONG.

RAIN, rain, and sun! a rainbow in the sky!
A young man will be wiser by and by:
An old man's wit may wander ere he
die :

Rain, rain, and sun! a rainbow on the lea!
And truth is this to me, and that to thee ;
And truth or clothed or naked let it be.

Rain, sun, and rain ! and the free blossom blows ;
Sun, rain, and sun ! and where is he who knows ?
From the great deep to the great deep he goes.

ENID'S SONG.

TURN, Fortune, turn thy wheel and lower
the proud;
Turn thy wild wheel thro' sunshine,
storm, and cloud;
Thy wheel and thee we neither love nor hate.

Turn, Fortune, turn thy wheel with smile or
frown;
With that wild wheel we go not up or down;
Our hoard is little, but our hearts are great.

Smile and we smile, the lords of many lands ;
Frown and we smile, the lords of our own hands ;
For man is man and master of his fate.

Turn, turn thy wheel above the staring crowd ;
Thy wheel and thou are shadows in the cloud ;
Thy wheel and thee we neither love nor hate.

VIVIEN'S SONG.

IN Love, if Love be Love, if Love be ours,
    Faith and unfaith can ne'er be equal
        powers:
Unfaith in aught is want ot faith in all.

It is the little rift within the lute,
That by and by will make the music mute,
And ever widening slowly silence all.

The little rift within the lover's lute,
Or little pitted speck in garner'd fruit,
That rotting inward slowly moulders all.

It is not worth the keeping : let it go :
But shall it ? answer, darling, answer, no.
And trust me not at all or all in all.

———

My name, once mine, now thine, is closelier mine,
For fame, could fame be mine, that fame were thine,
And shame, could shame be thine, that shame were
    mine,
So trust me not at all or all in all.

ELAINE'S SONG.

SWEET is true love tho' given in vain,
in vain ;
And sweet is death who puts an end
to pain :
I know not which is sweeter, no, not I.

Love, art thou sweet? then bitter death must be :
Love, thou art bitter ; sweet is death to me.
O Love, if death be sweeter, let me die.

Sweet love, that seems not made to fade away,
Sweet death, that seems to make us loveless clay,
I know not which is sweeter, no, not I.

I fain would follow love, if that could be ;
I needs must follow death, who calls for me ;
Call and I follow, I follow ! let me die.

SONG OF THE NOVICE.

LATE, late, so late! and dark the night
and chill!
Late, late, so late! but we can enter
still.
Too late, too late! ye cannot enter now.

No light had we: for that we do repent;
And learning this, the bridegroom will relent.
Too late, too late! ye cannot enter now.

No light: so late! and dark and chill the night!
O let us in, that we may find the light!
Too late, too late! ye cannot enter now.

Have we not heard the bridegroom is so sweet?
O let us in, tho' late, to kiss his feet!
No, no, too late! ye cannot enter now.

PRINTED BY VIRTUE AND CO., CITY ROAD, LONDON.

LIST OF BOOKS

PUBLISHED BY

STRAHAN AND CO.

Alford's (Dean) The New Tes-

tament. Authorised Version Revised. Long Primer
Edition, crown 8vo, 6s. ; Brevier Edition, fcap.
8vo, 3s. 6d.; Nonpariel Edition, small 8vo, 1s. 6d.

Essays and Addresses, chiefly

on Church Subjects. Demy 8vo, 7s. 6d.

The Year of Prayer;

being Family Prayers for the Christian Year.
Crown 8vo, 3s. 6d. ; small 8vo, 1s. 6d.

The Week of Prayer.

An Abridgment of "The Year of Prayer;" intended
for use in schools. Neat cloth, 9d.

Alford's (Dean) The Year of

Praise; being Hymns, with Tunes, for the Sundays and Holidays of the Year. Large type, with music, 3s. 6d.; without music, 1s. Small type, with music, 1s. 6d.; without music, 6d. Tonic Sol-fa Edition, crown 8vo, 1s. 6d.

How to Study the New Testa-

ment. Part I. The Gospels and the Acts.—II. The Epistles (first section).—III. The Epistles (second section) and the Revelation. Small 8vo, 3s. 6d. each.

Eastertide Sermons.

Small 8vo, 3s. 6d.

The Queen's English:

A Manual of Idiom and Usage. New and Enlarged Edition. Small 8vo, 5s.

Meditations:

Advent, Creation, and Providence. Small 8vo, 3s. 6d.

Letters from Abroad.

Crown 8vo, 7s. 6d.

Poetical Works.

New and Enlarged Edition. Crown 8vo, 5s.

Argyll's (The Duke of) The Reign

of Law. New Edition, with Additions. Crown 8vo, 6s. People's Edition, limp cloth, 2s. 6d.

Primeval Man.

An Examination of some Recent Speculations. Crown 8vo, 4s. 6d.

Iona.

With Illustrations. Crown 8vo, 3s. 6d.

Buchanan's (Robert) Idyls and

Legends of Inverburn. Crown 8vo, 6s.

London Poems.

Crown 8vo, 6s.

Undertones.

Small 8vo, 6s.

The Book of Orm.

Crown 8vo, 6s.

Ballads of Life, &c.

Crown 8vo.

Napoleon Fallen.

A Lyrical Drama. Crown 8vo, 3s. 6d.

M

Buchanan's (Robert) The Drama
of Kings. Crown 8vo, 12s.

Gladstone's (The Right Hon.W.
E.) On Ecce Homo. Crown 8vo, 5s.

Hare's (Augustus J. C.) Walks
in Rome. Second Edition. Two Vols. crown 8vo, 21s.

Hawthorne's (Nathaniel) English
Note-books. Edited by Mrs. Hawthorne. Two Vols. post 8vo, 24s.

French and Italian Note-books.
Two Vols. post 8vo, 24s.

Howson's (Dean) The Metaphors
of St. Paul. Crown 8vo, 3s. 6d.

The Companions of St. Paul.
Crown 8vo, 5s.

The Character of St. Paul.
Crown 8vo.

Hutton's (R. H.) Essays, Theo-
logical and Literary. Two Vols. square 8vo, 24s.

Legends of King Arthur and his
Knights of the Round Table (The). Compiled and
Edited by J. T. K. Small 8vo, sewed, 1s.;
cloth, 1s. 6d.

MacDonald's (George) Annals
of a Quiet Neighbourhood. Crown 8vo, 6s.

The Seaboard Parish.
Crown 8vo, 6s.

Dealings with the Fairies.
With Illustrations by Arthur Hughes. Square 32mo,
cloth gilt extra, 2s. 6d.

The Disciple and other Poems.
Crown 8vo, 6s.

Unspoken Sermons.
Crown 8vo, 3s. 6d.

The Miracles of Our Lord.
Crown 8vo, 5s.

At the Back of the North Wind.
With Illustrations. Crown 8vo, 7s. 6d.

Ranald Bannerman's Boyhood.
With Illustrations. Crown 8vo, 5s.

MacDonald's (George) The Prin-
cess and the Goblin. With Illustrations. Crown
8vo, cloth gilt extra.

Works of Fancy and Imagi-
nation : being a reprint of Poetical and other
Works. Pocket-volume Edition, in neat
case, £2 2s.

MacDonald's (Mrs. George)
Chamber Dramas for Children. Crown 8vo, 7s. 6d.

Macleod's (Norman, D.D.) Peeps
at the Far East. With Illustrations. Small 4to,
cloth gilt extra, 21s.

Eastward.
With Illustrations. Crown 8vo, 6s.

Billy Buttons, and other Cha-
racter Sketches. Post 8vo.

Thoughts on the Temptation
of Our Lord. Crown 8vo.

Job Jacobs and his Boxes.
In packets of Thirteen, 1s.

Macleod's (Norman, D.D.)
Parish Papers. Crown 8vo, 3s. 6d.

Reminiscences of a Highland
Parish. Crown 8vo, 6s.

Simple Truth spoken to Work-
ing People. Small 8vo, 2s. 6d.

The Earnest Student.
Being Memorials of John Mackintosh. Crown 8vo, 3s. 6d.

The Gold Thread.
A Story for the Young. With Illustrations. Square 8vo, 2s. 6d.

The Old Lieutenant and his
Son. With Illustrations. Crown 8vo, 3s. 6d.

The Starling.
With Illustrations. Crown 8vo, 6s.

Wee Davie.
Sewed, 6d.

Merivale's (Chas., B.D., D.C.L.)
Homer's Iliad. In English Rhymed Verse. Two Vols. demy 8vo, 24s.

Newman's (John Henry, D.D.)

Miscellanies from the Oxford Sermons, and other Writings. Crown 8vo, 6s.

Plumptre's (Professor) Biblical

Studies. Post 8vo, 7s. 6d.

Christ and Christendom :

Being the Boyle Lectures for 1866. Demy 8vo, 12s.

Lazarus, and other Poems.

Crown 8vo, 5s.

Master and Scholar, and other

Poems. Crown 8vo, 5s.

The Tragedies of Æschylos.

A New Translation, with a Biographical Essay, and an Appendix of Rhymed Choruses. Two Vols. crown 8vo, 12s.

The Tragedies of Sophocles.

A New Translation, with a Biographical Essay, and an Appendix of Rhymed Choruses. Crown 8vo, 7s. 6d.

Theology and Life.

Sermons chiefly on Special Occasions. Small 8vo, 6s.

Taylor's (Bayard) Faust.

A Tragedy. By Johann Wolfgang Von Goethe.
Translated in the original metres. Two Vols.
post 8vo, 28s.

Tennyson's (Alfred) Poems.

Small 8vo, 9s.

Maud, and other Poems.

Small 8vo, 5s.

In Memoriam.

Small 8vo, 6s.

The Princess.

Small 8vo, 5s.

Idylls of the King.

Small 8vo, 7s.—Collected, small 8vo, 12s.

Enoch Arden, &c.

Small 8vo, 6s.

The Holy Grail, and other

Poems. Small 8vo, 7s.

Library Edition of Mr. Tenny-

son's Works, in Five post 8vo. Vols., 10s. 6d.
each.

Tennyson's (Alfred) Pocket-

volume Edition of Mr. Tennyson's Works. Ten
Vols. 18mo, in neat case, 45s.; in extra bind-
ing, 50s.

Selections.

Square 8vo, cloth extra, 5s.; gilt edges, 6s.

Songs.

Square 8vo, cloth extra, 5s.

Concordance.

Crown 8vo, 7s. 6d.

Tennyson and Sullivan.—The

Window; or, the Songs of the Wrens. A Song-
cycle by Alfred Tennyson, with Music by
Arthur Sullivan. 4to, cloth gilt extra, 21s.

Warren's (John Leicester) Re-

hearsals : A Book of Verses. Crown 8vo, 6s.

Philoctetes.

A Metrical Drama after the Antique. Crown 8vo,
4s. 6d.

Orestes.

A Metrical Drama after the Antique. Crown 8vo,
4s. 6d.

STRAHAN & CO., 56, LUDGATE HILL.